SHORT STORIES OF VICTOR HUGO

Victor Hugo

SANAGE

PUBLISHING HOUSE

Paperback: 978-936205810-2
eBook: 978-936205743-3

Printed by:

Sanage Publishing House LLP
Mumbai, India

sanagepublishing@gmail.com

Victor Hugo (1802–1885) was a French writer and prominent figure during Europe's Romantic movement. As a child, he traveled across the continent due to his father's position in the Napoleonic army. As a young man, he studied law although his passion was always literature. In 1819, Hugo created Conservateur Littéraire, a periodical that featured works from up-and-coming writers. A few years later he published a collection of poems Odes et Poésies Diverses followed by the novel Han d'Islande in 1825. Hugo has an extensive catalog, yet he's best known for the classics The Hunchback of Notre-Dame (1831) and Les Misérables (1862).

Contents

A Fight With A Cannon

La vieuville was suddenly cut short by a cry of despair, and at the same time a noise was heard wholly unlike any other sound. The cry and sounds came from within the vessel.

The captain and lieutenant rushed toward the gun-deck but could not get down. All the gunners were pouring up in dismay.

Something terrible had just happened.

One of the carronades of the battery, a twenty-four pounder, had broken loose.

This is the most dangerous accident that can possibly take place on a shipboard. Nothing more terrible can happen to a sloop of was in open sea and under full sail.

A cannon that breaks its moorings suddenly becomes some strange, supernatural beast. It is a machine transformed into a monster. That short mass on wheels moves like a billiard-ball, rolls with the rolling of the ship, plunges with the pitching goes, comes, stops, seems to meditate, starts on its course again, shoots like an arrow from one end of the vessel to the other, whirls around, slips away, dodges, rears, bangs, crashes, kills, exterminates. It is a battering ram capriciously assaulting a wall. Add to this the fact that the ram is of metal, the wall of wood.

It is matter set free; one might say, this eternal slave was avenging itself; it seems as if the total depravity concealed in what we call inanimate things has escaped and burst forth all of a sudden; it appears to lose patience, and to take a strange mysterious revenge; nothing more relentless than this wrath of the inanimate. This enraged lump leaps like a panther, it has the clumsiness of an elephant, the nimbleness of a mouse, the obstinacy of an ox, the uncertainty of the billows, the zigzag of the lightning, the deafness of the grave. It weighs ten thousand pounds, and it rebounds like a child's ball. It spins and then abruptly darts off at right angles.

And what is to be done? How put an end to it? A tempest ceases, a cyclone passes over, a wind dies down, a broken mast can be replaced, a leak can be stopped, a fire extinguished, but what will become of this enormous brute of bronze. How can it be captured? You can reason with a bulldog, astonish a bull, fascinate a boa, frighten a tiger, tame a lion; but you have no resource against this monster, a loose cannon. You cannot kill it, it is dead; and at the same time, it lives. It lives with a sinister life which comes to it from the infinite. The deck beneath it gives it full swing. It is moved by the ship, which is moved by the sea, which is moved by the wind. This destroyer is a toy. The ship, the waves, the winds, all play with it, hence its frightful animation. What is to be done with this apparatus? How fetter this stupendous engine of destruction? How anticipate its comings and goings, its returns, its stops, its shocks? Any one of its blows on the side of the ship may stave it in. How foretell its frightful meanderings? It is dealing with a projectile, which alters its mind, which seems to have ideas, and changes its direction every instant. How check the course of what must be avoided? The horrible cannon struggles, advances, backs, strikes right, strikes left, retreats, passes by, disconcerts expectation, grinds up obstacles, crushes men like flies. All the terror of the situation is in the fluctuations of the flooring. How fight an inclined plane subject to caprices? The ship has, so to speak, in its belly, an imprisoned thunderstorm, striving to escape; something like a thunderbolt rumbling above an earthquake.

In an instant the whole crew was on foot. It was the fault of the gun captain, who had neglected to fasten the screw-nut of the mooring-chain and had insecurely clogged the four wheels of the gun carriage; this gave play to the sole and the framework, separated the two platforms, and the breeching. The tackle had given way, so that the cannon was no longer firm on its carriage. The stationary breeching, which prevents recoil, was not in use at this time. A heavy sea struck the port, the carronade, insecurely fastened, had recoiled and broken its chain, and began its terrible course over the deck.

To form an idea of this strange sliding, let one imagine a drop of water running over a glass.

At the moment when the fastenings gave way, the gunners were in the battery, some in groups, others scattered about, busied with the customary work among sailors getting ready for a signal for action. The carronade, hurled forward by the pitching of the vessel, made a gap in this crowd of men and crushed four at the first blow; then sliding back and shot out again as the ship rolled, it cut in two a fifth unfortunate, and knocked a piece of the battery against the larboard side with such force as to unship it. This caused the cry of distress just heard. All the men rushed to the companion-way. The gun-deck was vacated in a twinkling.

The enormous gun was left alone. It was given up to itself. It was its own master and master of the ship. It could do what it pleased. This whole crew, accustomed to laugh in time of battle, now trembled. To describe the terror is impossible.

Captain Boisberthelot and Lieutenant la Vieuville, although both dauntless men, stopped at the head of the companion-way and, dumb, pale, and hesitating, looked down on the deck below. Someone elbowed past and went down.

It was their passenger, the peasant, the man of whom they had just been speaking a moment before.

Reaching the foot of the companion-way, he stopped.

The cannon was rushing back and forth on the deck. One might have supposed it to be the living chariot of the Apocalypse. The marine lantern swinging overhead added a dizzy shifting of light and shade to the picture. The form of the cannon disappeared in the violence of its course, and it looked now black in the light, now mysteriously white in the darkness.

It went on in its destructive work. It had already shattered four other guns and made two gaps in the side of the ship, fortunately above the water-line, but where the water would come in, in case of heavy weather. It rushed frantically against the framework; the strong timbers withstood the shock; the curved shape of the wood gave them great power of resistance; but they creaked beneath the blows of this huge club, beating on all sides at once, with a strange sort of ubiquity. The percussions of a grain of shot shaken in a bottle are not swifter or more senseless. The four wheels passed back and forth over the dead men, cutting them, carving them, slashing them, till the five corpses were a score of stumps rolling across the deck; the heads of the dead men seemed to cry out; streams of blood curled over the deck with the rolling of the vessel; the planks, damaged in several places, began to gape open. The whole ship was filled with the horrid noise and confusion.

The captain promptly recovered his presence of mind and ordered everything that could check and impede the cannon's mad course to be thrown through the hatchway down on the gun-deck—mattresses, hammocks, spare sails, rolls of cordage, bags belonging to the crew, and bales of counterfeit assignats, of which the corvette carried a large quantity—a characteristic piece of English villainy regarded as legitimate warfare.

But what could these rags do? As nobody dared to go below to dispose of them properly, they were reduced to lint in a few minutes.

There was just sea enough to make the accident as bad as possible. A tempest would have been desirable, for it might have upset the cannon, and with its four wheels once in the air there would be some hope of getting it under control. Meanwhile, the havoc increased.

There were splits and fractures in the masts, which are set into the framework of the keel and rise above the decks of ships like great, round pillars. The convulsive blows of the cannon had cracked the mizzenmast and had cut into the mainmast.

The battery was being ruined. Ten pieces out of thirty were disabled; the breaches in the side of the vessel were increasing, and the corvette was beginning to leak.

The old passenger having gone down to the gun-deck, stood like a man of stone at the foot of the steps. He cast a stern glance over this scene of devastation. He did not move. It seemed impossible to take a step forward. Every movement of the loose carronade threatened the ship's destruction. A few moments more and a shipwreck would be inevitable.

They must perish or put a speedy end to the disaster; some course must be decided on; but what? What an opponent was this carronade! Something must be done to stop this terrible madness—to capture this lightning—to overthrow this thunderbolt.

Boisberthelot said to La Vieuville:

"Do you believe in God, chevalier?"

La Vieuville replied:

"Yes—no. Sometimes."

"During a tempest?"

"Yes, and in moments like this."

"God alone can save us from this," said Boisberthelot.

Everybody was silent, letting the carronade continue its horrible din.

Outside, the waves beating against the ship responded with their blows to the shocks of the cannon. It was like two hammers alternating.

Suddenly, in the midst of this inaccessible ring, where the escaped cannon was leaping, a man was seen to appear, with an iron bar in his hand. He was the author of the catastrophe, the captain of the gun, guilty of criminal carelessness, and the cause of the accident, the master of the carronade. Having done the mischief, he was anxious to repair it. He had seized the iron bar in one hand, a tiller-rope with a slip-noose in the other and jumped down the hatchway to the gun-deck.

Then began an awful sight; a Titanic scene; the contest between gun and gunner; the battle of matter and intelligence; the duel between man and the inanimate.

The man stationed himself in a corner, and, with bar and rope in his two hands, he leaned against one of the riders, braced himself on his legs, which seemed two steel posts; and livid, calm, tragic, as if rooted to the deck, he waited.

He waited for the cannon to pass by him.

The gunner knew his gun, and it seemed to him as if the gun ought to know him. He had lived long with it. How many times he had thrust his hand into its mouth! It was his own familiar monster. He began to speak to it as if it were his dog.

"Come!" he said. Perhaps he loved it.

He seemed to wish it to come to him.

But to come to him was to come upon him. And then he would be lost. How could he avoid being crushed? That was the question. All looked on in terror.

Not a breast breathed freely, unless perhaps that of the old man, who was alone in the battery with the two contestants, a stern witness.

He might be crushed himself by the cannon. He did not stir.

Beneath them the sea blindly directed the contest.

At the moment when the gunner, accepting this frightful hand-to-hand conflict, challenged the cannon, some chance rocking of the sea caused the carronade to remain for an instant motionless and as if stupefied. "Come, now!" said the man.

It seemed to listen.

Suddenly it leaped toward him. The man dodged the blow.

The battle began. Battle unprecedented. Frailty struggling against the invulnerable. The gladiator of flesh attacking the beast of brass. On one side, brute force; on the other, a human soul.

All this was taking place in semi-darkness. It was like the shadowy vision of a miracle.

A soul——strange to say, one would have thought the cannon also had a soul but a soul full of hatred and rage. This sightless thing seemed to have eyes. The monster appeared to lie in wait for the man. One would have at least believed that there was craft in this mass. It also chose its time. It was a strange, gigantic insect of metal, having or seeming to have the will of a demon. For a moment this colossal locust would beat against the low ceiling overhead, then it would come down on its four wheels like a tiger on its four paws and begin to run at the man. He, supple, nimble, expert, writhed away like an adder from all these lightning movements. He avoided a collision, but the blows which he parried fell against the vessel and continued their work of destruction.

An end of the broken chain was left hanging to the carronade. This chain had in some strange way become twisted about the screw of the cascabel. One end of the chain was fastened to the gun-carriage. The other, left loose, whirled desperately about the cannon, making all its blows more dangerous.

The screw held it in a firm grip, adding a thong to a battering-ram, making a terrible whirlwind around the cannon, an iron lash in a brazen hand. This chain complicated the contest.

However, the man went on fighting. Occasionally, it was the man who attacked the cannon; he would creep along the side of the vessel, bar and rope in hand; and the cannon, as if it understood, and as though suspecting some snare, would flee away. The man, bent on victory, pursued it.

Such things cannot long continue. The cannon seemed to say to itself, all of a sudden, "Come, now! Make an end of it!" and it stopped. One felt that the crisis was at hand. The cannon, as if in suspense, seemed to have, or really had—for to all it was a living being—a ferocious malice prepense. It made a sudden, quick dash at the gunner. The gunner sprang out of the way, let it pass by, and cried out to it with a laugh, "Try it again!" The cannon, as if enraged, smashed a carronade on the port side; then, again seized by the invisible sling which controlled it, it was hurled to the starboard side at the man, who made his escape. Three carronades gave way under the blows of the cannon; then, as if blind and not knowing what more to do, it turned its back on the man, rolled from stern to bow, injured the stern and made a breach in the planking of the prow. The man took refuge at the foot of the steps, not far from the old man who was looking on. The gunner held his iron bar in rest. The cannon seemed to notice it, and without taking the trouble to turn around, slid back on the man, swift as the blow of an axe. The man, driven against the side of the ship, was lost. The whole crew cried out with horror.

But the old passenger, till this moment motionless, darted forth more quickly than any of this wildly swift rapidity. He seized a package of counterfeit assignats, and, at the risk of being crushed, succeeded in throwing it between the wheels of the carronade. This decisive and perilous movement could not have been made with more exactness and precision by a man trained in all the exercises described in Durosel's "Manual of Gun Practice at Sea."

The package had the effect of a clog. A pebble may stop a log, the branch of a tree turn aside an avalanche. The carronade stumbled. The gunner, taking advantage of this critical opportunity, plunged his iron bar between the spokes of one of the hind wheels. The cannon stopped. It leaned forward. The man, using the bar as a lever, held it in equilibrium. The heavy mass was overthrown, with the crash of a falling bell, and the man, rushing with all his might, dripping with perspiration, passed the slipnoose around the bronze neck of the subdued monster.

It was ended. The man had conquered. The ant had control over the mastodon; the pygmy had taken the thunderbolt prisoner.

The mariners and sailors clapped their hands.

The whole crew rushed forward with cables and chains, and in an instant the cannon was secured.

The gunner saluted the passenger.

"Sir," he said, "you have saved my life."

The old man had resumed his impassive attitude and made no reply.

The man had conquered, but the cannon might be said to have conquered as well. An immediate shipwreck had been avoided, but the corvette was not saved. The damage to the vessel seemed beyond repair. There were five breaches in her sides, one, very large, in the bow; twenty of the thirty carronades lay useless in their frames. The one which had just been captured and chained again was disabled; the screw of the cascabel was sprung, and consequently leveling the gun made impossible. The battery was reduced to nine pieces. The ship was leaking. It was necessary to repair the damages at once, and to work the pumps.

The gun-deck, now that one could look over it, was frightful to behold. The inside of an infuriated elephant's cage would not be more completely demolished.

However great might be the necessity of escaping observation, the necessity of immediate safety was still more imperative to the corvette. They had been obliged to light up the deck with lanterns hung here and there on the sides.

However, all the while this tragic play was going on, the crew were absorbed by a question of life and death, and they were wholly ignorant of what was taking place outside the vessel. The fog had grown thicker; the weather had changed; the wind had worked its pleasure with the ship; they were out of their course, with Jersey and Guernsey close at hand, further to the south than they ought to have been, and in the midst of a heavy sea. Great billows kissed the gaping wounds of the vessel—kisses full of danger. The rocking of the sea threatened destruction. The breeze had become a gale. A squall, a tempest, perhaps, was brewing. It was impossible to see four waves ahead.

While the crew were hastily repairing the damages to the gun-deck, stopping the leaks, and putting in place the guns which had been uninjured in the disaster, the old passenger had gone on deck again.

He stood with his back against the mainmast.

He had not noticed a proceeding which had taken place on the vessel. The Chevalier de la Vieuville had drawn up the marines in line on both sides of the mainmast, and at the sound of the boatswain's whistle the sailors formed in line, standing on the yards.

The Count de Boisberthelot approached the passenger.

Behind the captain walked a man, haggard, out of breath, his dress disordered, but still with a look of satisfaction on his face.

It was the gunner who had just shown himself so skilful in subduing monsters, and who had gained the mastery over the cannon.

The count gave the military salute to the old man in peasant's dress, and said to him:

"General, there is the man."

The gunner remained standing, with downcast eyes, in military attitude.

The Count de Boisberthelot continued:

"General, in consideration of what this man has done, do you not think there is something due him from his commander?"

"I think so," said the old man.

"Please give your orders," replied Boisberthelot.

"It is for you to give them; you are the captain."

"But you are the general," replied Boisberthelot.

The old man looked at the gunner.

"Come forward," he said.

The gunner approached.

The old man turned toward the Count de Boisberthelot, took off the cross of Saint-Louis from the captain's coat and fastened it on the gunner's jacket.

"Hurrah!" cried the sailors.

The mariners presented arms.

And the old passenger, pointing to the dazzled gunner, added:

"Now, have this man shot."

Dismay succeeded the cheering.

Then in the midst of the death-like stillness, the old man raised his voice and said:

"Carelessness has compromised this vessel. At this very hour it is perhaps lost. To be at sea is to be in front of the enemy. A ship making a voyage is an army waging war. The tempest is concealed, but it is at hand. The whole sea is an ambuscade. Death is the penalty of any misdemeanor committed in the face of the enemy. No fault is reparable. Courage should be rewarded, and negligence punished."

These words fell one after another, slowly, solemnly, in a sort of inexorable metre, like the blows of an axe upon an oak.

And the man, looking at the soldiers, added:

"Let it be done."

The man on whose jacket hung the shining cross of Saint-Louis bowed his head.

At a signal from Count de Boisberthelot, two sailors went below and came back bringing the hammock-shroud; the chaplain, who since they sailed had been at prayer in the officers' quarters, accompanied the two sailors; a sergeant detached twelve marines from the line and arranged them in two files, six by six; the gunner, without uttering a word, placed himself between the two files. The chaplain, crucifix in hand, advanced and stood beside him. "March," said the sergeant. The platoon marched with slow steps to the bow of the vessel. The two sailors, carrying the shroud, followed. A gloomy silence fell over the vessel. A hurricane howled in the distance.

A few moments later, a light flashed, a report sounded through the darkness, then all was still, and the sound of a body falling into the sea was heard.

The old passenger, still leaning against the mainmast, had crossed his arms, and was buried in thought.

Boisberthelot pointed to him with the forefinger of his left hand, and said to La Vieuville in a low voice:

"La Vendée has a head."

Claude Gueux

Claude Gueux was a poor workman, living in Paris about eight years ago, with his mistress and child. Although his education had been neglected, and he could not even read, the man was naturally clever and intelligent, and thought deeply over matters. Winter came with its attendant miseries,—want of work, want of food, want of fuel. The man, the woman, and the child were frozen and famished. The man turned thief. I don't know what he stole. What signifies, as the result was the same: to the woman and child it gave three days' bread and warmth; to the man, five years' imprisonment. He was taken to Clairvaux,—the abbey now converted into a prison, its cells into dungeons, and the altar itself into a pillory. This is called progress.

Claude Gueux the honest workman, who turned thief from force of circumstances, had a countenance which impressed you,—a high forehead somewhat lined with care, dark hair already streaked with gray, deep-set eyes beaming with kindness, while the lower part clearly indicated firmness mingled with self-respect. He rarely spoke, yet there was a certain dignity in the man which commanded respect and obedience. A fine character, and we shall see what society made of it.

Over the prison workshop was an inspector, who rarely forgot that he was also a jailer to his subordinates, handing them the tools with one hand, and casting chains upon them with the other. A tyrant, never using even self-reasoning; with ideas against which there was no appeal; hard rather than firm, at times he could even be jocular,— doubtless a good father, a good husband, really not vicious, but bad.

He was one of those men who never can grasp a fresh idea, who apparently fail to be moved by an emotion; yet with hatred and rage in their hearts they look like blocks of wood, heated on the one side but frozen on the other. This man's chief characteristic was obstinacy; and so proud was he of this very stubbornness that he compared himself with Napoleon,—an optical delusion, like taking the mere flicker of a candle for a star. When he had made up his mind to do a thing, however absurd, he would carry out that absurd idea. How often it happens that, when a catastrophe occurs, if we inquire into the cause we find it originated through the obstinacy of one with little ability, but having full faith in his own powers.

Such was the inspector of the prison workshop at Clairvaux,—a man of flint placed by society over others, who hoped to strike sparks out of such material; but a spark from a like source is apt to end in a conflagration.

The inspector soon singled out Claude Gueux, who had been numbered and placed in the workshop, and finding him clever, treated him well. Seeing Claude looking sad (for he was ever thinking of her he termed his wife), and being in a good humour, by way of pastime to console the prisoner he told him the woman had become one of the unfortunate sisterhood and had been reduced to infamy; of the child nothing was known.

After a time, Claude had accustomed himself to prison rule, and by his calmness of manner and a certain amount of resolution clearly marked in his face, he had acquired a great ascendancy over his companions, who so much admired him that they asked his advice, and tried in all ways to imitate him. The very expression in his eyes clearly indicated the man's character; besides, is not the eye the window to the soul, and what other result could be anticipated than that the intelligent spirit should lead men with few ideas, who yielded to the attraction as the metal does to the loadstone? In less than three months Claude was the virtual head of the workshop, and at times he almost doubted whether he was king or prisoner, being treated something like a captive pope, surrounded by his cardinals.

Such popularity ever has as its attendant hatred; and though beloved by the prisoners, Claude was detested by the jailers. To him two men's rations would have been scarcely sufficient. The inspector laughed at this, as his own appetite was large; but what would be mirth to a duke, to a prisoner would be a great misfortune. When a free man, Claude Gueux could earn his daily four-pound loaf and enjoy it; but as a prisoner he daily worked, and for his labour received one pound and a half of bread and four ounces of meat; it naturally followed that he was always hungry.

He had just finished his meagre fare, and was about to resume his labours, hoping in work to forget famine, when a weakly-looking young man came towards him, holding a knife and his untasted rations in his hand, but seemingly afraid to address him.

"What do you want?" said Claude, roughly.

"A favour at your hands," timidly replied the young man.

"What is it?" said Claude.

"Help me with my rations; I have more than I can eat."

For a moment Claude was taken aback, but without further ceremony he divided the food in two and at once partook of one half.

"Thank you," said the young man; "allow me to share my rations with you every day."

"What is your name?" said Claude.

"Albin."

"Why are you here? "added Claude.

"I robbed."

"So did I," said Claude.

The same scene took place daily between this man old before his time (he was only thirty-six) and the boy of twenty, who looked at the most seventeen. The feeling was more like that of father and son than one brother to another; everything created a bond of union between them,—the very toil they endured together, the fact of sleeping in the same quarters and taking exercise in the same courtyard. They were happy, for were they not all the world to each other?

The inspector of the workshop was so hated by the prisoners that he often had recourse to Claude Gueux to enforce his authority; and when a tumult was on the point of breaking out, a few words from Claude had more effect than the authority of the warders. Although the inspector was glad to avail himself of this influence, he was jealous all the same and hated the superior prisoner with an envious and implacable feeling,—an example of might over right, all the more fearful as it was secretly nourished. But Claude cared so much for Albin that he thought little about the inspector.

One morning as the warders were going their rounds one of them summoned Albin, who was working with Claude, to go before the inspector.

"What are you wanted for?" said Claude.

"I do not know", replied Albin, following the warder.

All day Claude looked in vain for his companion, and at night, finding him still absent, he broke though his ordinary reserve and addressed the turnkey. "Is Albin ill?" said he.

"No," replied the man.

"How is it that he has never put in an appearance today?"

"His quarters have been changed," was the reply.

For a moment Claude trembled, then calmly continued, "Who gave the order?"

"Monsieur D____." This was the inspector's name.

On the following night the inspector, Monsieur D____, went his rounds as usual. Claude, who had perceived him from the distance, rose, and hastened to rasie his woollen cap and button his gray woolelen vest to the throat,—considered a mark of respect to superiors in prison discipline.

"Sir," said Claude, as the inspector was about to pass him, "has Albin really been quartered elsewhere?"

"Yes," replied the inspector.

"Sir, I cannot live without him. You know the rations are insufficient for me, and Albin divided his portion with me. Could you not manage to let him resume his old place near me?"

"Impossible; the order cannot be revoked."

"By whom was it given?"

"By me."

"Monsieur D_____," replied Claude, "on you my life depends."

"I never cancel an order once given."

"Sir, what have I done to you?"

"Nothing."

"Why, then," cried Claude, "separate me from Albin?"

"Because I do," replied the inspector, and with that he passed on.

Claude's head sank down, like the poor caged lion deprived of his dog; but the grief, though so deeply felt, in no way changed his appetite,—he was famished. Many offered to share their rations with him, but he steadily refused, and continued his usual routine in silence,—breaking it only to ask the inspector daily, in tones of anguish mingled with rage, something between a prayer and a threat, these two words: "And Albin?"

The inspector simply passed on, shrugging his shoulders; but had he only observed Claude he would have seen the evident change, noticable to all present, and he would have heard these words, spoken respectfully but firmly:——-

"Sir, listen to me; send my companion to me. It would be wise to do so, I can assure you. Remember my words!"

On Sunday he had sat for hours in the courtyard, with his head bowed in his hands, and when a prisoner called Faillette came up laughing, Claude said, "I am judging someone."

On the 25th of October 1831, as the inspector went his rounds, Claude, to draw his attention, smashed a watch-glass he had found in the passage. This had the desired effect.

"It was I," said Claude. "Sir, resore my comrade to me."

"Impossible," was the answer.

Looking the inspector full in the face, Claude firmly added: "Now, reflect! Today is the 25th of October; I give you till the 4th of November."

A warder remarked that Claude was threatening Monsieur D_____, and ought at once to be locked up.

"No, it is not a case of blackhole," replied the inspector, smiling disdainfully; "we must be considerate with people of this stamp."

The following day Claude was again accosted by one of the prisoners named Pernot, as he was brooding in the courtyard.

"Well, Claude, you are sad; indeed, what are you pondering over?"

"I fear some evil threatens that good Monsieur D_____," answered Claude.

Claude daily impressed the fact on the inspector how much Albin's absence affected him, but with no result save four-and-twenty hours' solitary confinement. On the 4th of November he looked round his cell for the little that remained to remind him of his former life. A pair of scissors, and an old volume of the "Emile," belonging to the woman he had loved so well, the mother of his child,—how useless to a man who could neither work nor read!

As Claude walked down the old cloisters, so dishonoured by its new inmates and its fresh whitewashed walls, he noticed how earnestly the convict Ferrari was looking at the heavy iron bars that crossed the window, and he said to him: "Tonight I will cut through those bars with these scissors, pointing to the pair he still held in his hand."

Ferrari laughed incredulously, and Claude joined in the mirth. During the day he worked with more than ordinary ardour, wishing to finish a straw hat, which he had been paid for in advance by a tradesman at Troyes,—M. Bressier.

Shortly before noon he made some excuse to go down into the carpenter's quarters, a story below his own, at the time the warders were absent. Claude received a hearty welcome, as he was equally popular here as elsewhere.

"Can anyone lend me an axe?" he said.

"What for?"

Without exacting any promises of secrecy, he at once replied: "To kill the inspector with tonight."

Claude was at once offered several; choosing the smallest, he hid it beneath his waistcoat and left. Now, there were twenty-seven prisoners present, and not one of those men betrayed him; they even refrained from talking upon the subject among themselves, waiting for the terrible event which must follow.

As Claude passed on he saw a young convict of sixteen yawning idly there, and he strongly advised him to learn how to read. Just then Faillette asked what he was hiding.

Claude answered unhestitatingly: "An axe to kill Monseiur D_____ tonight; but can you see it?"

"A little," said Faillette.

At seven o'clock the prisoners were locked in their several workshops. It was then the custom for the warders to leave them, until the inspector has been his rounds.

In Claude's workshop a most extraordinary scene took place, the only one of its kind on record. Claude rose and addressed his companions, eighty-four in number, in the following words:—

"You all know Albin and I were like brothers. I liked him at first for sharing his rations with me, afterwards because he cared for me. Now I never have sufficient, though I spend the pittance I earn in bread. It could make no possible difference to the inspector, Monsieur D_____, that we should be together; but he chose to separate us simply from a love of tormenting, for he is a bad man. I asked again and again for Albin to be sent back, without success; and when I gave him a stated time, the 4th of November, I was thrust into a dungeon. During that time, I became his judge and sentenced him to death on November the 4th. In two hours, he will be here, and I warn you I intend to kill him. But have you anything to say?"

There was dead silence. Claude then continued telling his comrades, the eighty-one thieves, his ideas on the subject,—that he was reduced to a fearful extremity, and compelled by that very necessity to take the law into his own hands; that he knew full well he could not take the inspector's life without sacrificing his own, but that as the cause was a just one he would bear the consequences, having come to the conclusion after two months' calm reflection; that if they considered resentment alone hurried him on to such a step they were at once to say so, and to state their objections to the sentence being carried out.

One voice alone broke the silence which followed, saying, "Before killing the inspector, Claude ought to give him a chance of relenting."

"That is but just," said Claude, "and he shall have the benefit of the doubt."

Claude then sorted the few things a poor prisoner is allowed and gave them to the comrades he mostly cared for after Albin, keeping only the pair of scissors. He then embraced them all,—some not being able to withhold their tears at such a moment. Claude continued calmly to converse during this last hour, and even gave way to a trick he had as a boy, of extinguishing the candle with a breath from his nose. Seeing him thus, his companions afterwards owned that they hoped he had abandoned his sinister idea. One young convict looked at him fixedly, trembling for the coming event.

"Take courage, young fellow," said Claude, gently; "it will be but the work of a minute."

The workshop was a long room with a door at both ends, and with windows each side overlooking the benches, thus leaving a pathway up the Centre for the inspector to review the work on both sides of him. Claude had now resumed his work, — something like Jacques Clement, who did not fail to repeat his prayers.

As the clock sounded the last quarter to nine, Claude rose and placed himself near the entrance, apparently calm. Amidst the most profound silence the clock struck nine; the door was thrown open, and the inspector came in as usual alone, looking quite jovial and self-satisfied, passing rapidly along, tossing his head at one, grinding words out to another, little heeding the eyes fixed so fiercely upon him. Just then he heard Claude's step, and turning quickly round said, —

"What are you doing here? Why are you not in your place?" just as he would have spoken to a dog.

Claude answered respectfully, "I wish to speak to you, sir."

"On what subject?"

"Albin."

"Again!"

"Always the same," said Claude.

"So then," replied the inspector, walking along, "you have not had enough with twenty-four hours in the blackhole."

Claude, following him closely, replied: "Sir, return my companion to me!"

"Impossible!"

"Sir," continued Claude, in a voice which would have moved Satan, I" implore you to send Albin back to me; you will then see how I will work. You are free, and it would matter but little to you; you do not know the feeling of having only one friend. To me it is everything, encircled by the prison walls. You can come and go at your pleasure; I have but Albin. Pray let him come back to me! You know well he shared his food with me. What can it matter to you that a man named Claude Gueux should be in this hall, having another by his side called Albin? You have but to say 'Yes,' nothing more. Sir, my good sir, I implore you, in the name of Heaven, to grant my prayer!"

Claude, overcome with emotion, waited for an answer.

"Impossible!" replied the inspector impatiently; "I will not recall my words. Now go, you annoyance!" And with that he hurried on towards the outer door, amidst the breathless silence maintained by eighty-one thieves.

Claude, following and touching the inspector, gently asked:" Let me at least know why I am condemned to death. Why did you separate us?"

"I have already answered you: because I chose," replied the inspector.

With that he was about to lift the latch, when Claude raised the axe, and without one cry the inspector fell to the ground, with his skull completely cloven from three heavy blows dealt with the rapidity of lightning. A fourth completely disfigured his face, and Claude, in his mad fury, gave another and a useless blow ; for the inspector was dead.

Claude, throwing the axe aside, cried out, "Now for the other!"

The other was himself; and taking the scissors, his wife's, he plunged them into his breast. But the blade was short, and the chest was deep, and vainly he strove to give the fatal blow. At last, covered with blood he fell fainting across the dead. Which of the two would be considered the victim?

When Claude regained consciousness he was in bed, surrounded by every care and covered with bandages. Near him were Sisters of Charity, and a recorder ready to take down his deposition, who with much interest inquired how he was. Claude had lost a great deal of blood; but the scissors had done him a bad turn, inflicting wounds not one of which was dangerous: the only mortal blows he had struck were on the body of Monsieur D____. Then the interrogatory commenced.

"Did you kill the inspector of the prison workshops at Clairvaux?"

"Yes," was the reply.

"Why did you do so?"

"Because I did."

Claude's wounds now assumed a more serious aspect, and he was prostrated with a fever which threatened his life. November, December, January, February passed, in nursing and preparations, and Claude in turn was visited by doctor and judge,—the one to restore him to health, the other to glean the evidence needful to send him to the scaffold.

On the 16th of March 1832, perfectly cured, Claude appeared in court at Troyes, to answer the charge brought against him. His appearance impressed the court favorably; he had been shaved and stood bareheaded, but still clad in prison garb. The court was well guarded by a strong military guard, to keep the witnesses within bounds, as they were all convicts. But an unexpected difficulty occurred; not one of these men would give evidence; neither questions nor threats availed to make them break their silence, until Claude requested them to do so. Then they in turn gave a faithful account of the terrible event; and if one, from forget-fullness or affection for the accused, failed to relate the whole facts, Claude supplied the deficiency. At one time the women's tears fell fast.

The usher now called the convict Albin. He came in trembling with emotion and sobbing painfully and threw himself into Claude's arms. Turning to the Public Prosecutor, Claude said, —

"Here is a convict who gives his food to the hungry," and stooping, he kissed Albin's hand.

All the witnesses having been examined, the counsel for the prosecution then rose to address the court. "Gentlemen of the jury, society would be utterly put to confusion if a public prosecution did not condemn great culprits like him, who, etc."

After the long address by the prosecution, Claude's counsel rose. Then followed the usual pleading for and against, whichever takes place at the criminal court.

Claude in his turn gave evidence, and everyone was astonished at his intelligence; there appeared far more of the orator about this poor workman than the assassin. In a clear and straightforward way, he detailed the facts as they were, — standing proudly there, resolved to tell the whole truth. At times the crowd was carried away by his eloquence. This man, who could not read, would grasp the most difficult points of argument, yet treat the judges with all due deference. Once Claude lost his temper, when the counsel for the prosecution stated that he had assassinated the inspector without provocation.

"What!" said Claude, "I had no provocation? Indeed! A drunkard strikes me, — I kill him; then you would allow there was provocation, and the penalty of death would be changed for that of the galleys. But a man who wounds me in every way during four years, humiliates me for four years, taunts me daily, hourly, for four years, and heaps every insult on my head,—what follows? You consider I have had no provocation! I had a wife for whom I robbed,—he tortured me about her. I had a child for whom I robbed,—he taunted me about this child. I was hungry, a friend shared his bread with me,—he took away my friend. I begged him to return my friend to me,—he cast me into a dungeon. I told him how much I suffered,—he said it wearied him to listen. What then would you have me do? I took his life; and you look upon me as a monster for killing this man, and you decapitate me: then do so."

Provocation such as this the law fails to acknowledge, because the blows have no marks to show.

The judge then summed up the case in a clear and impartial manner,—dwelling on the life Claude had led, living openly with an improper character; then he had robbed, and ended by being a murderer. All this was true. Before the jury retired, the judge asked Claude if he had any questions to ask, or anything to say.

"Very little," said Claude. " I am a murderer, I am a thief; but I ask you gentlemen of the jury, why did I kill? Why did I steal?"

The jury retired for a quarter of an hour, and according to the judgment of these twelve countrymen—gentlemen of the jury, as they are styled—Claude Gueux was condemned to death. At the very outset several of them were much impressed with the name of Gueux (vagabond), and that influenced their decision.

When the verdit was pronounced, Claude simply said: "Very well; but there are two questions these gentlemen have not answered. Why did this man steal? What made him a murderer?"

He made a good supper that night, exclaiming, "Thirty-six years have now passed me." He refused to make any appeal until the last minute, but at the instance of one of the sisters who had nursed him he consented to do so. She in her fulness of heart gave him a five-franc piece.

His fellow prisoners, as we have already noticed, were devoted to him, and placed all the means at their disposal to help him to escape. They threw into his dungeon, through the air-hole, a nail, some wire, the handle of a pail: any one of these would have been enough for a man like Claude to free himself from his chains. He gave them all up to the warder.

On the 8th of June 1832, seven months and four days after the murder, the recorder of the court came, and Claude was told that he had but one hour more to live, for his appeal had been rejected.

"Indeed," said Claude coldly; "I slept well last night, and doubtless I shall pass my next even better."

First came the priest, then the executioner. he was humble to the priest, and listened to him with great attention, regretting much that he had not had the benefit of religious training, at the same time blaming himself for much in the past.

He was courteous in his manner to the executioner; in fact, he gave up all,—his soul to the priest, his body to the executioner.

While his hair was being cut, someone mentioned how the cholera was spreading, and Troyes at any moment might become prey to this fearful scourge. Claude joined in the conversation, saying, with a smile, "There is one thing to be said,—I have no fear of the cholera!" He had broken half of the scissors,—what remained he asked the jailer to give to Albin; the other half lay buried in his chest. He also wished the day's rations to be taken to his friend. The only trifle he retained was the five-franc piece that the sister had given him, which he kept in his right hand after he was bound.

At a quarter to eight, the dismal procession usual in such cases left the prison. Pale, but with a firm tread, Claude Gueux slowly mounted the scaffold, keeping his eyes fixed on the crucifix the priest carried,—an emblem of the Savior's suffering. He wished to embrace the priest and the executioner, thanking the one and pardoning the other; the executioner simply repulsed him. Just before he was bound to the infernal machine, he gave the five-franc piece to the priest, saying, "For the poor."

The hour had scarcely struck its eight chimes, when this man, so noble, so intelligent, received the fatal blow which severed his head from his body.

A market-day had been chosen for the time of execution, as there would be more people about, for there are still in France small towns that glory in having an execution. The guillotine that day remained, inflaming the imagination of the mob to such an extent that one of the tax-gatherers was nearly murdered. Such is the admirable effect of public executions!

We have given the history of Claude Gueux's life, more to solve a difficult problem than for aught else. In his life there are two questions to be considered,—before his fall, and after his fall. What was his training, and what was the penalty? This must interest society generally; for this man was well gifted, his instincts were good. Then what was wanting? On this revolves the grand problem which would place society on a firm basis.

What nature has begun in the individual, let society carry out. Look at Claude Gueux. An intelligent and most noble-hearted man, placed in the midst of evil surroundings, he turned thief. Society placed him in a prison where the evil was yet greater, and he ended up becoming a murderer. Can we really blame him, or ourselves?——questions which require deep thought, or the result will be that we shall be compelled to shirk this most important subject. The facts are now before us, and if the government gives no thought to the matter, what are the rulers about?

The Deputies are yearly much occupied. It is important to shift sinecures and to unravel the budget; to pass an Act which compels me, disguised as a soldier, to mount guard at the Count de Lobau's whom I do not know, and to whom I wish to remain a stranger, or to go on a parade under the command of my grocer, who has been made an officer. I wish to cast no reflections on the patrol, who keep order and protect our homes, but on the absurdity of making such parade and military hubub about turning citizens into parodies of soldiers.

Deputies or ministers! it is important that we should sound every subject, even though it end in nothing; that we should question and cross-question what we know but little about. Rulers and legislators! you pass your time in classical comparisons that would make a village schoolmaster smile. You assert that it is the habits of modern civilization that have engendered adultery, incest, parricide, infanticide, and poisoning,——proving that you know little of Jocasta, Phedra, Oedipus, Medea, or Rodoguna. The great orators occupy themselves in lengthy discussions on Corneille and Racine and get so heated in literary argument as to make the grossest mistakes in the French language. Very important indeed all this is, but we consider there are subjects of far greater consequence. In the midst of such useless arguments, what answer would the Deputies give if one rose and gravely addressed them in the following words:——-

"Silence, all those who have been speaking! silence, I say! You consider yourself acquainted with the question? You know nothing about it. The question is this: In the name of justice, scarcely a year ago, a man at Panners was cut to pieces; at Dijon a woman's head was taken off; in Paris, at St. Jacques, executions take place without number. This is the question! Now take your time to consider it, you who argue over the buttons of the National Guards, whether they should be white or yellow, and if security is preferable to certainty!

"Gentlemen of the Right, gentlemen of the Left, the great mass of the people suffer! Whether a republic or a monarchy, the fact remains the same,—the people suffer! The people are famished, the people are frozen. Such misery leads them to crime: the galleys take the sons, houses of ill-fame the daughters. You have too many convicts, too many unfortunates.

"What is the meaning of this social gangrene? You are near the patient: treat the malady. You are at fault; now study the matter more deeply.

"When you pass laws, what are they but expedients and palliatives? Half your codes result from routine.

"Branding but cauterizes the wound, and it mortifies, and what is the end? You stamp the crime for life on the criminal; you make two friends of them, two companions — inseparables. The convict prison is a blister which spreads far worse matter than ever it extracts; and as for the sentence of death, when carried out it is a barbarous amputation. Therefore, branding, penal servitude, and sentence of death are all of one class; you have done away with the branding, banish the rest. Why keep the chain and the chopper now you have put aside the hot iron? Farinace was atrocious, but he was not ridiculous.

"Take down that worn ladder that leads to crime and to suffering. Revise your laws; revise your codes; rebuild your prisons; replace your judges. Make laws suited to the present time.

"You are bent on economy; do not be so lavish in taking off the heads of so many during the year. Suppress the executioner; you could defray the expenses of six hundred schoolmasters with the wages you give your eighty executioners. Think of the multitude; then there would be schools for the children, workshops for the men.

"Do you know that in France there are fewer people who know how to read than in any other country in Europe? Fancy, Switzerland can read, Belgium can read, Denmark can read, Greece can read, Ireland can read — and France cannot read! It is a crying evil.

"Go into our convict prisons, examine each one of these condemned men, and you will observe by the profile, the shape of the head, how many could find their type in the lower animals. Here are the lynx, the cat, the monkey, the vulture, the hyena. Nature was first to blame, no doubt; but the want of training fostered the evil. Then give the people a fair education, and what there is of good in these ill-conditioned minds, let that be developed. people must be judged by their opportunities. Rome and Greece were educated; then brighten the people's intellect.

"When France can read, then give the people encouragement for higher things. Ignorance is preferable to a little ill-directed knowledge; and remember, there is a book of far greater importance than the 'Compere Mathieu,' more popular than the 'Constitutionnel,' and more worthy of perusal than the charter of 1830,—that is the Bible.

"Whatever you may do for the people, the majority will always remain poor and unhappy. Theirs the work, the heavy burden to carry, to endure: all the miseries for the poor, all the pleasures for the rich.

"As such is life, ought not the State to lean to the weaker and helpless side?

"In the midst of all this wretchedness, if you but throw hope in the balance, let the poor man learn there is a heaven where joy reigns, a paradise that he can share, and you raise him; he feels that he has a part in the rich man's joys. And this was the teaching Jesus gave, and He knew more about it than Voltaire.

"Then give to those people who work, and who suffer here, the hope of a different world to come, and they will go on patiently; for patience but follows in the footsteps of hope.

"Then spread the Gospel in all our villages, let every cottage have its Bible; the seed thus sown will soon circulate. Encourage virtue, and from that will spring so much that now lies fallow.

"The man turned assassin under certain circumstances, if differently influenced would have served his country well.

"Then give the people all encouragement; improve the masses, enlighten them, guard their morals, make them useful, and to such heads as those you will not require to use cold steel."

The Vicissitudes of Civil War

Around him suddenly, from all directions, the thicket was filled with muskets, bayonets, and sabres, a tricolored banner was unfurled in the dim light, and the cry, "Lantenac!" burst forth on his ears, while at his feet through the brambles and branches savage faces appeared.

The Marquis was standing alone on the top of the height, visible from every part of the wood. He could scarcely distinguish those who shouted his name, but he could be seen by all. Had there been a thousand muskets in the wood, he offered them a target. He could distinguish nothing in the coppice, but the fiery eyes of all were directed upon him.

He took off his hat, turned back the brim, and drawing from his pocket a white cockade, he pulled out a long dry thorn from a furze-bush, with which he fastened the cockade to the brim of his hat, then replaced it on his head, the upturned brim revealing his forehead and the cockade, and in a loud voice, as though addressing the wide forest, he said:—

"I am the man you seek. I am the Marquis de Lantenac, Viscount de Fontenay, Breton Prince, Lieutenant-General of the armies of the king. Make an end of it. Aim! Fire!"

And opening with both hands his goat-skin waistcoat, he bared his breast.

Lowering his eyes to see the levelled guns, he beheld himself surrounded by kneeling men.

A great shout went up,—"Long live Lantenac! Long live our lord! Long live the General!"

At the same time hats were thrown up and sabres whirled joyously, while from all sides brown woollen caps hoisted on long poles were waving in the air.

A Vendean band surrounded him.

At the sight of him they fell on their knees.

Legends tell us that the ancient Thuringian forests were inhabited by strange beings,—a race of giants, at once superior and inferior to men,—whom the Romans regarded as horrible beasts, and the Germans as divine incarnations, and who might chance to be exterminated or worshipped according to the race they encountered.

A sensation similar to that which may have been felt by one of those beings was experienced by the Marquis when, expecting to be treated like a monster, he was suddenly worshipped as a deity.

All those flashing eyes were fastened upon him with a kind of savage love.

The crowd were armed with guns, sabres, scythes, poles, and sticks. All wore large felt hats or brown caps, with white cockades, a profusion of rosaries and charms, wide breeches left open at the knee, jackets of skin, and leather gaiters; the calves of their legs were bare, and they wore their hair long; some looked fierce, but all had frank and open countenances.

A young man of noble bearing passed through the crowd of kneeling men and hastily approached the Marquis. He wore a felt hat with an upturned brim, a white cockade, and a skin jacket, like the peasants; but his hands were delicate, and his linen was fine, and over his waistcoat was a white silk scarf, from which hung a sword with a golden hilt.

Having reached the hure, he threw aside his hat, unfastened his scarf, and kneeling, presented to the Marquis both scarf and sword.

"Indeed, we were seeking for you," he said, "and we have found you. Receive the sword of command. These men are yours now. I was their commander; now I am promoted, since I become your soldier. Accept our devotion, my lord. General, give me your orders."

At a sign from him, men carrying the tricolored banner came forth from the woods, and going up to the Marquis, placed it at his feet. It was the one he had seen through the trees.

"General," said the young man who presented the sword and the scarf, "this is the flag which we took from the Blues who held the farm Herbe-en-Pail. My name is Gavard, my lord. I was with the Marquis de la Rouarie."

"Very well," said the Marquis.

And calm and composed he girded on the scarf.

Then he pulled out his sword, and waving it above his head, he cried,—

"Rise! And long live the king!"

All started to their feet. Then from the depth of the woods arose a tumultuous and triumphant cry,—

"Long live the king! Long live our Marquis! Long live Lantenac!"

The Marquis turned towards Gavard.

"How many are you?"

"Seven thousand."

While they were descending the hill, the peasants clearing away the furze-bushes to make a path for the Marquis de Lantenac, Gavard continued:—

"All this may be explained in a word, my lord: nothing could be more simple. It needed but a spark. The republican placard in revealing your presence has roused the country for the king. Besides, we have been secretly notified by the mayor of Granville, who is one of us,—the same who saved the Abbé Ollivier. They rang the tocsin last night."

"For whom?"

"For you."

"Ah!" said the Marquis.

"And here we are," continued Gavard.

"And you number seven thousand?"

"To-day. But we shall be fifteen thousand to-morrow. It is the Breton contingent. When Monsieur Henri de la Rochejaquelein went to join the catholic army they sounded the tocsin, and in one night six parishes—Isernay, Corqueux, Échaubroignes, Aubiers, Sainte Aubin and Nueil—sent him ten thousand men. They had no munitions of war, but having found at a quarryman's house sixty pounds of blasting-powder, Monsieur de la Rochejaquelein took his departure with that. We felt sure you must be somewhere in these woods, and we were looking for you."

"And you attacked the Blues at the farm Herbe-en-Pail?"

"The wind prevented them from hearing the tocsin, and they mistrusted nothing; the population of the hamlet, a set of clowns, received them well. This morning, we invested the farm while the Blues were sleeping, and the thing was over in a trice. I have a horse here; will you deign to accept it, general?"

"Yes."

A peasant led up a white horse with military housings. The Marquis mounted him without accepting Gavard's proffered assistance.

"Hurrah!" cried the peasants. The English fashion of cheering is much in vogue on the Breton coast, for the people have continual dealings with the Channel islands.

Gavard made the military salute, asking, as he did so, "Where will you establish your headquarters, my lord?"

"At first, in the forest of Fougères."

"It is one of the seven forests belonging to you."

"We need a priest."

"We have one."

"Who is it?"

"The curate of the Chapelle-Erbrée."

"I know him. He has made the trip to Jersey." A priest stepped out from the ranks and said,—

"Three times."

The Marquis turned his head.

"Good morning, Monsieur le Curé. There is work in store for you."

"So much the better, Monsieur le Marquis."

"You will have to hear the confessions of such as desire your services. No one will be forced."

"Marquis," said the priest, "at Guéménée, Gaston compels the republicans to confess."

"He is a hairdresser. The dying should be allowed free choice in such a matter."

Gavard, who had gone away to give certain orders, now returned.

"I await your commands, general."

"In the first place, the rendez-vous is in the forest of Fougères. Direct the men to separate and meet there."

"The order has been given."

"Did you not say that the people of Herbe-en-Pail were friendly to the Blues?"

"Yes, general."

"Was the farm burned?"

"Yes."

"Did you burn the hamlet?"

"No."

"Burn it."

"The Blues tried to defend themselves. But they numbered one hundred and fifty, while we were seven thousand."

"What Blues are they?"

"Those of Santerre."

"He who ordered the drums to beat while they were beheading the king? Then it is a Parisian battalion?"

"A demi-battalion."

"What was it called?"

"Their banner has on it, 'Battalion of the Bonnet-Rouge.'"

"Wild beasts."

"What is to be done with the wounded?"

"Put an end to them."

"What are we to do with the prisoners?"

"Shoot them."

"There are about eighty of them."

"Shoot them all."

"There are two women."

"Treat them all alike."

"And three children."

"Bring them along. We will decide what Is to be done with them."

And the Marquis spurred his horse forward.

www.ingramcontent.com/pod-product-compliance
Lightning Source LLC
La Vergne TN
LVHW041443170726
843492LV00008B/2784